Lot No. 249

*A Mummy Horror Classic –
Reanimation, Revenge, and Academic
Intrigue*

A Modern Translation

Adapted for the Contemporary Reader

Arthur Conan Doyle

Translated by Tim Zengerink

Table of Contents

Preface - Message to the Reader

What If You Could Help Rebuild the Greatest Library in Human History?

Thousands of years ago, the Library of Alexandria stood as the crown jewel of human achievement — a sanctuary where the collected wisdom of every known civilization was gathered, preserved, and shared freely.

And then, it was lost.

Through fire, conquest, and the slow erosion of time, humanity lost not just books — but ideas, dreams, discoveries, and stories that could have changed the world forever.

Today, the Library of Alexandria lives again — and you are invited to be a part of its restoration.

Our mission is simple yet profound:

To rebuild the greatest library the world has ever known, and to translate all timeless works into every language and dialect, so that no seeker of knowledge is ever left behind again.

By joining our movement to rebuild the modern Library of Alexandria, you become part of an unprecedented mission:

- **Unlimited Access to the Greatest Audiobooks & eBooks Ever Written:**

  Instantly explore thousands of legendary works—Plato, Shakespeare, Jane Austen, Leo Tolstoy, and countless more. All instantly available to read or listen, placing a complete literary universe at your fingertips.

- **Beautiful Paperback & Deluxe Editions at Printing Cost**

  Own any title as an elegant paperback, deluxe hardcover, or stunning collectible boxset—offered to you at true printing cost, delivered straight to your door. Build your personal Library of Alexandria, crafted for beauty, built for durability, and worthy of proud display.

- **Fresh Translations for Modern Readers—in Every Language & Dialect**

  Enjoy timeless masterpieces reimagined in clear, contemporary language—no more outdated phrases or obscure references. Alongside the original versions, we're tirelessly translating these classics into every language and dialect imaginable, ensuring accessibility and understanding across cultures and generations.

- **Join a Global Renaissance of Literature & Knowledge**

  You directly support expanding our library, publishing deluxe editions at true cost, translating works into all global languages, and bringing humanity's greatest stories to people everywhere. By joining today, you're not just preserving a legacy of masterpieces; you set in motion a powerful wave of literary accessibility.

Become a Torchbearer of Knowledge.

Join us for free now at **LibraryofAlexandria.com**

Together, we will ensure that the light of human wisdom never fades again.

With gratitude and a shared love of knowledge,

The Modern Library of Alexandria Team

Visit:

www.libraryofalexandria.com

Or scan the code below:

Introduction

Victorian Egyptomania, Academic Rivalry, and the Birth of the Mummy Horror Genre

Arthur Conan Doyle's Lot No. 249, first published in 1892, holds the distinctive honor of being the earliest known literary work to feature a reanimated Egyptian mummy as a figure of supernatural horror. Predating Universal Studios' iconic 1932 film The Mummy by four decades, Doyle's tale serves as the foundational template for an entire subgenre of horror fiction. Yet despite its historical importance, Lot No. 249 is far more than just a genre originator. It is a tightly woven, atmospherically rich story of academic rivalry, occult revenge, and imperial fascination with ancient civilizations.

Set in the gothic halls of Oxford University, the story centers on Abercrombie Smith, a medical student whose rational worldview is challenged when his neighbor's bizarre behavior and strange experiments culminate in inexplicable occurrences. The neighbor in question, Edward Bellingham, is a recluse, scholar of Egyptology, and owner of a mysterious auction item:

Lot No. 249 — an authentic Egyptian mummy. When those who cross Bellingham begin to experience terrifying attacks by a silent, shadowy assailant, Smith begins to suspect that the ancient corpse may be more than just an artifact. The resulting tale is equal parts detective story and supernatural thriller, tinged with Doyle's unique blend of rationalism and gothic imagination.

In classic Conan Doyle fashion, the story is presented with a sense of empirical detail, as though the narrator were describing a case from the annals of medical or legal history. This technique grounds the more fantastic elements of the plot in an atmosphere of credibility, making the horrors that unfold feel both immediate and plausible. Doyle, always a master of suspense, builds tension through suggestion, restraint, and the use of reliable witnesses whose sanity and intelligence heighten the believability of the supernatural.

In this introduction, we will explore Lot No. 249 in three primary dimensions: its place within the cultural context of Victorian Egyptomania and imperial anxiety; its use of science, skepticism, and academia as frameworks for horror; and its role in establishing the mummy as a figure of literary fear. We will uncover how Doyle transforms ancient myth into modern dread, and how the story's seemingly narrow scope conceals profound questions about power, knowledge, and the limits of rational control.

The Allure and Anxiety of the Ancient World

To fully appreciate the cultural impact of Lot No. 249, it is essential to understand the historical phenomenon of Egyptomania that swept through Britain during the 19th century. Following Napoleon's campaigns in Egypt and the subsequent British colonial presence there, Western fascination with ancient Egypt became a widespread obsession. Mummies, tombs, hieroglyphics, and curses captivated the Victorian imagination, feeding into both scholarly inquiry and public spectacle. Museums showcased human remains as curiosities. Archaeologists became celebrities. And the mysteries of Egypt offered a paradoxical mix of admiration and fear.

Doyle, deeply embedded in the intellectual and imperial circles of his time, captures this cultural moment with uncanny precision. Bellingham, the story's antagonist, embodies the dark side of academic Egyptology: the figure who goes too far, who seeks not only to understand the past, but to control it. His studies are not purely scholarly. They veer into the arcane, the ritualistic, and the profane. He violates the boundary between study and sorcery.

In Bellingham, Doyle offers a subtle critique of imperial arrogance. The idea that a British scholar can uncover and command ancient forces speaks to the colonial mindset—a belief in the right to possess and dominate other cultures. But Lot No. 249 turns this belief on its head. The mummy, once awakened, does not serve. It punishes. It becomes an avenger, an embodiment of the past's refusal to be reduced to mere academic property.

The figure of the mummy, then, is not just a monster. It is a symbol of historical reckoning. It rises not to terrify randomly, but to redress violations. This is what gives Doyle's tale its moral force. Beneath the suspense lies a powerful subtext: that the dead, when disturbed, may not forgive the living.

Reason vs. the Unexplainable: Academia as Gothic Battleground

One of the most intriguing aspects of Lot No. 249 is its setting. Rather than a castle, crypt, or distant desert, the story unfolds in the hallowed corridors of Oxford. This environment—revered as a seat of reason, knowledge, and discipline—becomes the unlikely stage for supernatural terror. By placing the horror within a scholarly community, Doyle explores the tension between empirical rationalism and the unexplainable.

Abercrombie Smith, the protagonist, is a quintessential man of science. He is disciplined, skeptical, and values logic above all else. His initial reaction to Bellingham's eccentricities is irritation, not fear. Even as strange events occur—phantom movements, inexplicable injuries, and signs of arcane rituals—Smith clings to the belief that all phenomena must have a rational explanation.

But Doyle deftly erodes this confidence. Bit by bit, the limits of Smith's understanding are tested. He sees evidence that cannot be dismissed, hears sounds that defy explanation, and ultimately witnesses actions that no science can account for. His confrontation with the truth is not one of willing conversion, but of reluctant acknowledgment. In this way, Doyle uses Smith to dramatize a broader Victorian crisis: the recognition that science, for all its power, cannot encompass the full range of human experience.

At the same time, the story raises questions about knowledge without wisdom. Bellingham, for all his learning, is morally bankrupt. His curiosity is divorced from conscience. The horror he unleashes is not the result of ignorance, but of knowing too much and caring too little. Thus, Doyle situates the true danger not in the supernatural itself, but in the misuse of learning—a warning that resonates deeply in a modern world increasingly shaped by unchecked technological advancement.

The Mummy Awakened: Horror, Symbolism, and Literary Legacy

What makes Lot No. 249 so historically significant is its role in birthing a new kind of monster. While vampires, ghosts, and werewolves had long haunted the pages of Western literature, the Egyptian mummy had not yet been imagined as a source of terror. Doyle's innovation was to take a cultural fascination and infuse it with dread, creating a template that would influence horror fiction for generations.

The mummy in this story is not a lumbering brute or a tragic victim. It is silent, precise, and implacable. Doyle never allows it to speak, and rarely describes it in full. This restraint makes the creature more terrifying. It moves in darkness, appears at windows, and leaves bruises on the necks of its victims. It is a presence rather than a character, a force rather than a personality. And it obeys only Bellingham's will—until, perhaps, it does not.

The ambiguity surrounding the mummy's autonomy adds an additional layer of horror. Is it merely a tool of revenge, or does it possess its own sense of justice? The story suggests that once awakened, such ancient forces cannot be fully controlled. They may begin as instruments, but they end as arbiters.

This concept would become central to the mummy genre in later decades, from films like The Mummy (1932) to modern retellings. Doyle established the archetype: the disturbed dead returning not randomly, but purposefully, to punish sacrilege and hubris. In doing so, he created a monster that is both exotic and familiar, both ancient and terrifyingly present.

Lot No. 249 also exemplifies Doyle's broader literary vision: the blending of mystery with metaphysics, of suspense with spirituality. His fascination with the unknown, which would later lead him to embrace spiritualism, finds here an early and masterful expression. The story neither confirms nor denies the supernatural. It suggests, disturbs, and invites. And in that space between certainty and fear, it achieves its greatest power.

As you read this modern translation, consider what still lies buried beneath our assumptions—about science, empire, history, and justice. For some tombs, Doyle reminds us, are not meant to be opened. And once opened, they are never silent again.

Lot No. 249

No one may ever truly understand what happened between Edward Bellingham and William Monkhouse Lee—or what caused Abercrombie Smith's deep fear. Yes, we have Smith's full account of the events, backed up by his servant Thomas Styles, Reverend Plumptree Peterson from Old's College, and a few others who saw bits and pieces of what happened. Still, most of the story depends on Smith alone. People might find it easier to believe that even a seemingly sane person like Smith had a flaw in his mind, rather than accept that the natural laws of the world were broken in a respected place like Oxford University. But when we remember how narrow and unclear the path of nature really is— how little we actually understand, even with all our science—it doesn't seem impossible that someone might wander down a strange and dark road we can't explain.

In one wing of what we'll call Old College at Oxford, there's a very old tower room. The stone arch over its entrance has bent with age, and the grey stone blocks are covered in lichen and held together with ivy, as if nature itself was trying to keep the building from falling apart. A winding stone staircase leads up from the door, curving past two floors before ending at a third. The steps have been worn smooth and uneven by centuries of students climbing them in search of knowledge. So many lives have passed over them—students from the time of the Plantagenets to more modern college boys—yet now, all those dreams and passions are gone, remembered only by names carved into old gravestones and maybe a bit of dust in a coffin. Still, the silent staircase and old grey walls remain, covered in faded symbols and carvings from the past.

In May of 1884, three students lived in the rooms along that old staircase. Each room had a study and a bedroom. On the ground floor were two other rooms—one used to store coal and the other lived in by the servant, Thomas Styles, who helped care for the students upstairs. These rooms were surrounded on both sides by lecture halls and offices, giving the tower a quiet, secluded feel that serious students liked. The ones living there at that time were Abercrombie Smith on the top floor, Edward Bellingham below him, and William Monkhouse Lee on the first floor.

It was 10 o'clock on a clear spring night. Abercrombie Smith was relaxing in an armchair with his feet up and his pipe in his mouth. His old school friend, Jephro Hastie, sat across from him in another chair.

Both were wearing their sports clothes—they had spent the evening rowing on the river. Anyone who looked at their strong, sharp faces could tell they were athletic, outdoorsy types. Hastie was the lead rower for his college team, and Smith was an even better rower, though his upcoming exams had kept him focused on studying, with only a few hours a week for physical activity. The cluttered table full of medical books, bones, models, and diagrams showed how serious he was about his studies. Above the fireplace hung two wooden training sticks and a pair of boxing gloves, showing how he stayed in shape with Hastie's help. The two friends were so comfortable with each other that they could sit quietly together without needing to speak—a true sign of close friendship.

"Want some whisky?" Smith asked at last, blowing out a puff of smoke. "There's Scotch in the jug and Irish in the bottle."

"No thanks," said Hastie. "I'm training for the sculling race. I don't drink while I'm in training. What about you?"

"I'm studying hard. I think it's best to skip it."

Hastie nodded, and they went back to their peaceful silence.

"By the way," Hastie said after a while, "have you met either of the guys living on your stair yet?"

"Just nodded at them in passing. That's it."

"Hm. I'd keep it that way if I were you. I know a little about them. Not much, but enough. I wouldn't try to get close. Not that there's anything really wrong with Monkhouse Lee."

"You mean the thin one?"

"Exactly. He's polite and decent. I don't think there's anything bad about him personally. But you can't know him without also knowing Bellingham."

"You mean the heavy guy?"

"Yeah, the big one. And he's someone I'd rather stay away from."

Abercrombie Smith raised his eyebrows and looked over at his friend.

"What's wrong with him?" he asked. "Drinking? Gambling? Just a jerk? You never used to be so judgmental."

"You must not know him well, or you wouldn't ask. There's something creepy about him—like a snake. He gives me the chills. I'd guess he has some dark secrets.

He's not dumb, though. They say he's one of the best students the college has ever had in his field."

"What's he studying? Medicine or history?"

"Eastern languages. He's amazing at them. Chillingworth saw him last year near the second cataract of the Nile, and said he spoke with the locals like he was born there. He used Coptic with the Copts, Hebrew with the Jews, Arabic with the Bedouins—everyone treated him like royalty. Even the strange old hermits who usually hiss and spit at strangers fell at his feet. Chillingworth couldn't believe it. And Bellingham acted like he expected it—walking around like he was their master. Not bad for a student at Old's College, huh?"

"So why did you say you can't know Lee without knowing Bellingham?"

"Because Bellingham is engaged to Lee's sister, Eveline. She's such a sweet girl, Smith. I know her and her whole family well. It's awful seeing her with that guy. They look like a dove and a toad when they're together."

Smith grinned and tapped the ashes out of his pipe against the fireplace.

"You're really letting your feelings show, old man," he said. "Jealousy, maybe? You don't actually have any real reason to hate the guy."

"Well, I've known Eveline since she was about the size of that pipe. I don't want to see her take a dangerous chance. And being with him is a risk. He looks awful. He has a terrible temper, too—mean and nasty. Do you remember what happened with Long Norton?"

"No, I'm new here. You keep forgetting I'm a freshman."

"Oh right, it was last winter. You know that path along the river? A few students were walking there, Bellingham in the lead, when they came across an old market woman walking the other way. It had rained a lot, and the path was squeezed between the river and a huge puddle. Instead of stepping aside, Bellingham just kept going and shoved the poor woman into the mud— ruined her and all her goods. It was a disgusting thing to do, and Long Norton—who's one of the nicest guys you'll meet—called him out. They argued, and Norton ended up hitting Bellingham with his walking stick. There was a big fuss afterward, and now whenever Bellingham sees Norton, he gives him a look that could kill. Anyway—wow—it's nearly eleven!"

"No rush. Light your pipe again."

"Can't. I'm supposed to be training. And here I've been, gossiping instead of sleeping. Hey, can I borrow your skull? Williams has had mine forever. I'll take the little ear bones too, if you're not using them. Thanks. Don't worry about a bag—I can carry them under my arm. Good night, and take my advice about your neighbor."

After Hastie clattered down the old staircase, carrying the bones, Abercrombie Smith tossed his pipe into the trash, pulled his chair closer to the lamp, and opened a big green book filled with colorful diagrams of the human body—the strange and complex "kingdom" we all live in but don't fully control. He was new to Oxford, but not new to medicine. He had already studied four years in Glasgow and Berlin. This next exam would officially make him a doctor. He had a strong face, a firm jaw, and a wide forehead. He wasn't flashy, but he was determined and hardworking—someone who might one day surpass people with more raw talent just through persistence. If you can hold your own in both Scotland and Germany, you're not someone who gives up easily. Smith had earned respect in both places, and now he was focused on doing the same at Oxford through sheer hard work.

He read for about an hour. The ticking carriage clock on the table showed it was nearly midnight when he suddenly heard a sharp, high-pitched sound—like someone gasping deeply, full of emotion. Smith set down his book and listened. No one lived above or beside him, so the sound must have come from the room below—Bellingham's room, the one Hastie had spoken so badly about.

Smith only knew Bellingham as a pale, quiet man who studied late. Even after Smith turned off his own lamp, Bellingham's would still shine through the old turret window. That shared habit of staying up late had quietly connected them. Smith liked knowing someone else was awake nearby when the hours dragged on. Even now, thinking of him, Smith felt no anger. Hastie was a good guy, but he was tough and not very imaginative. He didn't have much patience for anyone who didn't fit his idea of a "proper man." He often confused someone's health with their character— blaming weakness on bad morals instead of poor circulation. Smith, who had a broader view, understood his friend's attitude and kept it in mind as he thought again of the quiet man below him.

There were no more strange sounds, and Smith was just about to go back to his studies when suddenly a loud, harsh scream shattered the silence. It was the kind of scream someone lets out when they're completely overwhelmed by fear. Smith jumped out of his chair and dropped his book. He was usually calm and collected, but something about that scream made his skin crawl.

It came at such a strange time and place that his mind started racing with wild thoughts. Should he run downstairs, or stay where he was? He didn't want to cause a scene, and he didn't know his neighbor well enough to go barging in. He stood there, unsure what to do—when suddenly he heard fast footsteps on the stairs. Then Monkhouse Lee, only half dressed and pale as a ghost, burst into his room.

"Come quick!" he gasped. "Bellingham's sick!"

Smith followed him straight downstairs into the room below his. Even though he was focused on helping, he couldn't help but be stunned by what he saw. It looked more like a museum than a student's room. The walls and ceiling were covered with strange items from Egypt and the East. Tall, weird figures carrying things or holding weapons were painted around the room. Above them were statues with heads like bulls, storks, cats, and owls. Some had snakes on their heads and eyes shaped like almonds. Statues of Egyptian gods like Horus, Isis, and Osiris sat on every shelf and in every corner. Hanging from the ceiling was a huge crocodile, its mouth wide open, tied up in ropes.

In the middle of the room was a large square table, cluttered with papers, bottles, and dried leaves from some kind of palm plant. Everything had been pushed aside to make space for a mummy case, which had clearly been moved from its spot on the wall. The mummy—blackened, shriveled, and terrifying—was halfway out of the case, with one claw-like hand resting on the table. An old yellow scroll of papyrus was propped up against the case. In front of it sat Bellingham in a wooden chair. His head was thrown back, his eyes wide open in terror, staring at the crocodile above him. His lips were puffing out with each shaky breath.

"Oh no—he's dying!" cried Lee in panic.

Lee was a slim, good-looking young man with dark eyes and tan skin—he looked more Spanish than English. His emotional intensity was the complete opposite of Smith's calm nature.

"I don't think it's that bad," said Smith, who was studying medicine. "Help me lift him. You take his feet. Let's get him on the sofa. Knock off those little wooden idols, will you? What a mess! Okay, now let's loosen his collar and splash some water on him. He should come around soon. What was he even doing?"

"I don't know," Lee said. "I heard him yell and ran up. I know him pretty well. It's really kind of you to come help."

"His heart's racing like crazy," Smith said, pressing his hand to Bellingham's chest. "He looks scared out of his mind. Throw some more water on him. That face— what a look!"

It truly was an awful sight. His face wasn't just pale—it was bone-white, like the underside of a fish. He was very fat, but it looked like he used to be even bigger. His loose skin sagged in folds, crisscrossed with wrinkles. His short brown hair stuck up, and his big, wrinkled ears stuck out. His pale gray eyes were still open, wide with fear. Smith had never seen anyone look so completely terrified. He started to take Hastie's earlier warning more seriously.

"What on earth could have scared him like this?" Smith asked.

"It's the mummy."

"The mummy? What do you mean?"

"I don't know. It's disgusting and weird. I wish he'd give it up. This is the second time he's scared me like this. The same thing happened last winter. I found him just like this, staring at that creepy thing."

"Why is he even messing around with a mummy?"

"He's obsessed with this stuff—it's his hobby. He knows more about ancient Egypt than anyone else in

England. But still, I wish he'd stop. Wait—he's starting to wake up."

Bellingham's pale cheeks were slowly turning pink again. His eyelids trembled. He clenched and unclenched his hands, then took a deep, shaky breath. Suddenly, he sat up, looked around, and when he saw the mummy, he jumped off the sofa, grabbed the papyrus scroll, shoved it into a drawer, locked it, and collapsed back onto the couch.

"What's going on?" he asked. "What are you two doing here?"

"You were screaming like crazy," said Lee. "If our upstairs neighbor hadn't come down, I don't know what I would've done."

"Oh—it's Abercrombie Smith," said Bellingham, glancing up. "Thanks for coming. What a fool I am! Oh, what an idiot!"

He dropped his head into his hands and burst into loud, uncontrollable laughter.

"Hey—cut it out!" Smith said firmly, shaking his shoulder. "Your nerves are shot. You have to stop playing with mummies in the middle of the night or you're going to lose your mind. You're completely on edge right now."

"I wonder," Bellingham said, "if you'd be as calm as I am after seeing what I saw—"

"What did you see?"

"Oh... nothing. I just mean... maybe staying up with a mummy all night would get to anyone. You're probably right. I've overdone it lately. But I'm okay now. Please stay a few more minutes until I feel back to normal."

"The air in here's awful," said Lee, opening the window to let in the cool night breeze.

"It's balsamic resin," Bellingham said. He picked up one of the dried, palm-shaped leaves from the table and held it over the lamp. As it burned, thick smoke rose into the air, filling the room with a strong, sharp smell. "It's a sacred plant—used by the ancient priests," he added. "Do you know anything about Eastern languages, Smith?"

"Not at all. I don't know a single word," Smith replied.

Bellingham seemed relieved by the answer.

"By the way," he asked, "how long was I unconscious?"

"Only about four or five minutes."

"I figured it wasn't long," Bellingham said, taking a deep breath. "But when you're unconscious, time feels weird. I couldn't tell if I was out for a few seconds or for days. Now, that guy on the table—he was wrapped up during the 11th dynasty, around four thousand years ago. And if he could talk, he'd probably say it felt like he just blinked. He's a pretty impressive mummy, Smith."

Smith walked over to look at the body, using his medical knowledge to study it. Even though the face was badly discolored, the features were still clear. Two tiny, nut-like eyes sat deep inside the dark eye sockets. The skin was tightly stretched over the bones, and rough black hair hung over the ears. Two thin teeth stuck out from under the dried lips. The mummy was curled up with bent limbs and a forward-leaning head, which gave it an unsettling look—like it still held some life. The ribs poked through the leathery skin, the stomach had caved in and turned grayish-blue, and there was a long cut left by the embalmer. The legs were still wrapped in yellow cloth. Pieces of dried herbs like myrrh and cassia were scattered around the body and inside the coffin.

"I don't know his name," Bellingham said, gently touching the mummy's dry head. "The outer coffin with all the writing is missing. He's just called Lot 249 now—

you can see the number printed on the case. That's the number from the auction where I bought him."

"He must've been a good-looking man once," Smith said.

"He was a giant. The mummy is six-foot-seven, which is very tall for someone from that time. People back then were usually smaller. Look at these huge bones—he must've been tough."

"Maybe those hands helped build the pyramids," Monkhouse Lee said, clearly disgusted by the mummy's long, twisted fingers.

"No chance," Bellingham replied. "This guy was preserved with natron and carefully taken care of. Regular workers didn't get that kind of treatment—they were just buried with salt or tar. Experts say this kind of mummification would cost around 730 pounds in today's money. So he had to be someone important— probably a nobleman. What do you think that writing near his feet means, Smith?"

"I told you, I don't know any Eastern languages."

"Ah, right. I think it's the name of the embalmer. He must've been very skilled. I wonder how many things made today will still exist four thousand years from now."

Bellingham kept talking fast and casually, but Smith could tell he was still scared. His hands were shaking, his bottom lip trembled, and he kept glancing nervously back at the mummy. Still, there was a strange sense of satisfaction in his voice. His eyes looked excited, and he walked around the room with quick steps. It was like he had been through something terrifying, but it had helped him reach his goal.

"You're not leaving already, are you?" Bellingham asked as Smith stood up.

When he realized Smith was really going, he looked nervous again and reached out to stop him.

"I have to go. I've got work to do," Smith said. "You're okay now. Honestly, with the way your nerves are, you should choose a hobby that's a little less creepy."

"Oh, I'm not usually nervous. I've unwrapped mummies before."

"You fainted last time," Monkhouse Lee reminded him.

"Yeah, I guess I did," Bellingham admitted. "Maybe I need something for my nerves—or a shock of electricity. Lee, are you heading out too?"

"I'll do whatever you want, Ned."

"Then I'll come with you and sleep on your couch tonight. Good night, Smith. Sorry again for the trouble."

They shook hands, and as Smith walked back up the twisting stairs, he heard a key turn in the door below, followed by the sound of Bellingham and Lee heading down to the lower floor.

***

That's how Edward Bellingham and Abercrombie Smith first got to know each other—though Smith didn't really want to be friends. Bellingham, however, seemed to like his straightforward neighbor and kept trying to be friendly in ways that Smith couldn't easily turn down without being rude. He came by twice to thank Smith for helping him, and after that, he often dropped in with books, articles, or small neighborly favors.

Smith soon realized that Bellingham was very smart. He read a lot, was interested in all kinds of topics, and had an excellent memory. He was also polite and pleasant to talk to, and over time, his creepy looks became less noticeable. Even though Smith was cautious at first, he eventually started to enjoy their chats and even visited Bellingham now and then.

Still, something about Bellingham didn't sit right with Smith. Even though he was clearly intelligent, there was something strange—maybe even a little unhinged—about him. Every so often, he would say things that were way too dramatic for someone living such a quiet life.

"It feels amazing," he once said, "to have the power to do great good or terrible harm—to be like an angel or a demon." Another time, he said about Monkhouse Lee, "Lee's kind and honest, but he's weak. He has no ambition. He couldn't keep up with someone like me who's working on something big."

When Bellingham made weird comments like that, Smith would just raise his eyebrows and puff on his pipe, replying with dry advice like, "Try some fresh air," or "You should get to bed earlier."

There was something else that bothered Smith: Bellingham had started talking to himself a lot. Late at night, when there was no one visiting, Smith could hear a soft, mumbling voice coming from the room below his. The whispers were faint but clearly there, and they annoyed Smith enough that he mentioned them a couple of times. But Bellingham always denied it and got strangely defensive, more upset than the situation called for.

Smith wasn't the only one who noticed something odd. Tom Styles, the old servant who had worked in the building longer than anyone could remember, also had concerns.

"Excuse me, sir," he said one morning while cleaning Smith's room. "Do you think Mr. Bellingham is... well, alright in the head?"

"What makes you ask?" Smith replied.

"Well, sir, he's changed. He's not like he used to be. And honestly, sir, he was never quite like Mr. Hastie or yourself. But now he talks to himself constantly. I don't know how it doesn't bother you. I just don't know what to make of him anymore."

"That's not really your business, Styles," Smith said.

"You're right, sir," Styles said. "But I do care. I've looked after a lot of young men here. I kind of feel responsible for them. And when something bad happens, I'm the one who has to face their families. But there's one more thing, sir. Sometimes I hear something moving around in Bellingham's room when he's not even home—and the door's locked."

"What? That's nonsense, Styles."

"Maybe it is, sir. But I know what I heard."

"That's ridiculous."

"Very good, sir. Just ring if you need me."

Smith didn't give Styles' warning much thought. But a few days later, something strange happened that made him remember it clearly.

Bellingham had come by late at night to chat and was telling Smith about some rock tombs in Upper Egypt. As Smith listened—his hearing was very sharp—he suddenly heard the sound of a door opening on the floor below.

"Someone just went into or out of your room," he said.

Bellingham jumped up, looking shocked and nervous. "I'm sure I locked it. I thought I locked it," he said quickly. "No one should be able to open it."

"I think someone's coming upstairs now," Smith said.

Bellingham rushed out, slamming the door behind him, and ran down the stairs. Smith heard him stop halfway and thought he caught a bit of whispering. A few seconds later, the door downstairs closed, a key turned in the lock, and Bellingham came back up, pale and sweating.

"It's fine," he said, dropping into a chair. "It was just my dog. He must've pushed the door open. I must've forgotten to lock it."

"I didn't know you had a dog," Smith said, giving him a careful look.

"I just got him. He's kind of a handful. I might need to get rid of him."

"He must be a smart dog if he can open a closed door. Wouldn't just shutting it be enough?"

"I'm trying to stop Styles from letting him out. He's valuable, and I can't afford to lose him."

"I like dogs," Smith said, still watching him. "Maybe I could see him sometime."

"Sure. But not tonight—I have an appointment. Is that clock right? I'm already fifteen minutes late. Sorry, I've got to run."

Bellingham grabbed his cap and left in a hurry. But despite what he said, Smith clearly heard him go back into his own room and lock the door from the inside.

That conversation left Smith feeling uncomfortable. Bellingham had clearly lied to him—and not even well. It was obvious he was hiding something important. Smith knew for a fact that Bellingham didn't own a dog. And whatever he had heard on the stairs that night hadn't sounded like an animal at all. So what was it? He remembered what old Styles had said about hearing something walking around the room when Bellingham wasn't even home. Could it have been a woman? Smith thought that might be possible. If so, and the university found out, Bellingham could be expelled. That could explain why he was so nervous and why he lied. Still, it was hard to imagine anyone hiding a woman in a college room without being caught. Whatever the real reason was, Smith didn't like it. He decided to stay distant and stop Bellingham from trying to get closer.

But his study session didn't last long that night. He had just started to focus again when heavy footsteps came up the stairs. Hastie burst into the room wearing his blazer and workout clothes.

"Still working?" he said, dropping into his usual chair. "You'd probably keep reading even if an earthquake hit Oxford! Don't worry, I won't stay long. Just here for a few puffs on my pipe."

"What's the news?" Smith asked, packing tobacco into his pipe.

"Not much. Wilson scored 70 for the freshmen against the main team. They're thinking about putting him in instead of Buddicomb. Buddicomb's lost his edge—can't bowl to save his life anymore. Just sends out weak shots now."

"Medium right?" Smith asked seriously.

"Leaning toward fast, with a leg twist. Used to be tricky on wet ground. Oh, and speaking of news—have you heard about Long Norton?"

"What happened?"

"He got attacked."

"Attacked?"

"Yeah. It happened just as he was leaving the High Street, about a hundred yards from Old's gate."

"But who attacked him?"

"That's the thing! If you asked 'what' instead of 'who,' you might be closer to the truth. Norton swears it wasn't human. And judging by the scratches on his neck, I might believe him."

"What are you saying? Ghosts?" Smith asked, sounding skeptical.

"Not exactly. But maybe some showman lost a big ape or something. If that beast's still loose around here, it could be behind the attack. Norton walks the same path every night. There's a low-hanging tree there—he thinks the thing dropped on him from the branches. It grabbed him around the neck with arms as strong and thin as steel cables. He didn't see it, just felt those arms squeezing tighter and tighter. He screamed like crazy until two guys came running, and whatever it was jumped the wall like a cat. Norton never got a good look. But it really shook him up. I joked that it was better than a vacation for him."

"Probably just a mugger," Smith said.

"Could be. But Norton says it wasn't. The guy had long nails and could jump like a pro. And by the way, your charming neighbor would probably be happy to hear about it. He's got a grudge against Norton, and he doesn't seem like the type to let things go. But hey—what's with that look on your face?"

"Nothing," Smith said quickly.

He had jumped in his chair, and a flash of worry crossed his face—like something troubling had just hit him.

"You looked like something I said really bothered you. Oh—and didn't you meet Bellingham since I last came by? Monkhouse Lee told me you did."

"Yeah. I've seen him a couple of times."

"Well, you're big enough to take care of yourself. But he's not exactly what I'd call a healthy character. Smart, sure—but not someone I'd trust. Lee's fine, though. Good guy. Anyway, I've got to go. I'm rowing against Mullins for the Vice-Chancellor's Cup next

Wednesday. Make sure you come watch if I don't see you before then."

Smith set down his pipe and tried to get back to his books. But no matter how hard he tried, he couldn't concentrate. His thoughts kept drifting back to Bellingham and the weird mystery surrounding him. Then he thought about the attack Hastie had described—and the rumor that Bellingham held a grudge against the victim. Those two thoughts kept coming back together, as if they were somehow connected. But the idea was so vague and shadowy that he couldn't even explain it to himself.

"Damn that guy," Smith muttered, tossing his pathology book across the room. "He's ruined my night's work. If I needed another reason to stay away from him, this is it."

For the next ten days, Smith stayed completely focused on his studies. He didn't see or hear anything from either of the men living below him. During the times Bellingham used to drop by, Smith made sure to keep his outer door closed. Even when someone knocked, he ignored it.

But one afternoon, as he was heading downstairs, Bellingham's door suddenly flew open. Monkhouse Lee stormed out with a furious look on his face and his eyes blazing. Right behind him came Bellingham, red-faced and shaking with anger.

"You idiot!" Bellingham hissed. "You'll regret this."

"Maybe," Lee snapped, "but I don't care. It's over. I won't be part of it!"

"You promised!" Bellingham growled.

"I'll keep my promise! I won't say anything. But I'd rather see Eva dead than let this go on. It's over. She'll do what I say. And we never want to see you again."

Smith heard that as he walked by, but he didn't stop. He had no interest in getting involved. It was obvious something serious had happened between them. Lee clearly wanted to end his sister's engagement to Bellingham. Smith remembered Hastie's description of Bellingham as a toad and Eva as a dove, and he felt relieved it was finally over. Bellingham's angry face wasn't one a girl could trust. As Smith walked away, he wondered what had started the fight—and what promise Bellingham had tried to force Monkhouse Lee to keep.

That day was the big rowing match between Hastie and Mullins, and lots of students were walking toward the river to watch. The sun was shining, and the elm trees cast long shadows across the road. The old stone college buildings stood quietly, as if watching all the young students pass by. Teachers in black robes, serious scholars, and tan athletes in colorful jackets all headed toward the river.

Smith, who knew rowing well, picked a spot where he thought the race would get intense. He heard the starting cheer in the distance, followed by louder shouts and the sound of feet running. A group of breathless runners raced past. Smith leaned forward and saw Hastie rowing steadily, with Mullins trailing behind. He cheered for his friend, checked his watch, and was about to leave when someone tapped his shoulder. It was Monkhouse Lee.

"I saw you," Lee said, a little nervous. "Can we talk for a bit? That cottage over there is mine—I share it with Harrington from King's. Want to come in for some tea?"

"I really should get back soon," said Smith. "I'm deep in study mode. But sure, I can come in for a few minutes. I only came out to support Hastie."

"He's my friend too," Lee said. "He rows beautifully. Mullins didn't stand a chance. Come on—it's a small place, but it's nice for studying in summer."

The cottage was small and white, with green shutters and a wooden porch. It stood about fifty yards from the river. Inside, the room was simple—a table, bookshelves, and a few cheap pictures on the wall. A kettle boiled on a small stove, and tea was ready on a tray.

"Sit down and have a smoke," said Lee. "I'll pour the tea. Thanks for coming—I know you're busy. I just wanted to tell you something. If I were you, I'd move out of your room right away."

"What?" Smith said, surprised, with a lit match in one hand and an unlit cigarette in the other.

"I know it sounds strange. And the worst part is, I can't tell you why—I promised. But I can say this: I don't think it's safe to live near Bellingham. That's why I plan to stay out here for a while."

"Not safe? What do you mean?"

"That's the part I can't explain. But trust me— please move. We had a huge argument today. You must've heard it when you were coming down the stairs."

"I saw you two fighting."

"He's awful, Smith. That's the only word for him. I've had a bad feeling ever since that night he fainted— you remember when you came down to check on him? Today, I called him out, and he told me some things that really scared me. Then he tried to get me to help him. I'm not super strict or anything, but I was raised by a clergyman. And there are some things I just won't go near. I'm just glad I found out before it was too late. He was going to marry into my family."

"That's quite a statement," Smith said seriously. "But it feels like you're either saying too much or not enough."

"I'm just warning you."

"If this warning is serious, a promise shouldn't stop you from explaining. If someone was about to set off a bomb, I wouldn't let a promise stop me from stopping him."

"But I can't stop him. All I can do is warn you."

"Without saying what the warning is about?"

"Just stay away from Bellingham."

"That's not helpful. Why should I be afraid of him?"

"I can't tell you. But I really think you should move. I'm not saying he wants to hurt you—just that he's dangerous to be around right now."

"Maybe I know more than you think," said Smith, staring at him. "What if I told you someone else is living in Bellingham's room?"

Lee jumped to his feet in shock.

"So you know?" he gasped.

"A woman."

Lee dropped back into his chair and groaned.

"I can't say anything," he said. "I made a promise."

"Well," said Smith, standing up, "I'm not going to let fear push me out of a room I like. It would be silly to move out just because you say Bellingham might do something. I think I'll stay put. And since it's almost five, I need to get going."

He said a quick goodbye to the young student and walked home through the warm spring evening. He felt a mix of irritation and amusement—like anyone would after being warned about something mysterious and unclear.

No matter how busy he was, Abercrombie Smith always made time for one thing. Twice a week, on Tuesdays and Fridays, he walked to Farlingford, where Doctor Plumptree Peterson lived, about a mile and a half from Oxford. Peterson had been close friends with Smith's older brother Francis, and since he was a well-off bachelor with a great wine collection and a better library, Smith enjoyed visiting. Each time, Smith would take a fast walk down country roads and then relax for an hour in Peterson's cozy study, chatting over a glass of port about college news or the latest in medicine.

The day after talking to Monkhouse Lee, Smith closed his books at 8:15 p.m.—his usual time to leave for Peterson's. As he was heading out, he noticed a book on his desk that Bellingham had lent him. His conscience bothered him. Even if Bellingham wasn't pleasant, it was rude not to return the book. He picked it up and went downstairs to return it. He knocked on the door, and when no one answered, he tried the handle. It was unlocked. Glad to avoid another awkward meeting, he stepped inside, left the book and his card on the table, and looked around.

The lamp was turned down low, but Smith could still see the room clearly. Everything looked just as it had before—the Egyptian drawings, the statues with animal heads, the crocodile hanging from the ceiling, and the messy table covered with papers and dried leaves. The mummy case stood upright against the wall—but the mummy was gone. The room seemed empty otherwise. As Smith left, he thought maybe he'd been wrong about Bellingham. If he really had a secret, why would he leave his door unlocked?

The narrow spiral stairs were pitch black as Smith made his way down. Then, suddenly, he felt like something had moved past him. It was just a small sound, a faint breeze, something brushing against his elbow—but it was so light, he couldn't be sure. He stopped and listened. The wind rustled outside in the ivy, but he heard nothing more.

"Styles, is that you?" he called out.

No answer. Everything was quiet again. It must've been a draft—old buildings like this had cracks everywhere. Still, Smith felt like he'd heard footsteps right next to him.

He walked into the courtyard, still thinking about it, when someone ran toward him across the grass.

"Smith, is that you?" the man called.

"Hastie!" Smith replied.

"Thank God! You need to come, now! Monkhouse Lee just drowned. Harrington from King's brought the news. The doctor's not around—you'll have to do. Maybe he's still alive!"

"Do you have brandy?" Smith asked.

"No."

"I have some upstairs. There's a flask on my table."

Smith raced back up the stairs, skipping three at a time. He grabbed the flask and was on his way down when he passed Bellingham's room—and froze.

The door, which he had closed earlier, was now wide open. And in the middle of the room, lit by the lamp, stood the mummy case. Just minutes ago, it had been empty—he was sure of it. But now, the mummy was inside it. Its thin, dried body stood stiff and tall, with its black, wrinkled face turned toward the door. It looked dead, yet somehow... Smith felt like there was still some spark of life in those deep, hollow eyes.

He was so stunned he forgot why he was rushing. He just stared at the creepy figure—until Hastie's voice snapped him out of it.

"Come on, Smith! It's life or death! Hurry!"

Smith shook himself and ran downstairs. "Let's sprint," Hastie said. "It's under a mile. We can make it in five minutes. A human life is worth the run!"

They ran side by side through the night and didn't stop until they reached the riverside cottage. Inside, Monkhouse Lee lay limp and wet on the sofa, like a water-soaked plant. Green slime clung to his dark hair, and white foam covered his lips. Harrington knelt beside him, rubbing his arms, trying to bring him back.

"I think he's still alive," said Smith, putting his hand on Lee's chest. "Check his breath with a watch glass... Yes, there's a little fog. Grab one arm, Hastie, and do what I do. We'll get him breathing."

For ten minutes, they worked in silence, pushing and pulling on Lee's chest. At last, his body twitched, his lips moved, and his eyes slowly opened. The three students let out a loud cheer.

"Wake up, man! You really scared us."

"Here—drink some brandy."

"He'll be okay now," said Harrington. "I got such a shock. I was reading here and went out for a quick walk when I heard a scream and a splash. I ran to the river and found him, but he looked dead. Simpson couldn't find a doctor—his leg's injured—so I had to run. I don't know what I would've done without you guys. That's it, sit up."

Monkhouse Lee slowly pushed himself up with shaky arms, looking around in confusion.

"What happened?" he asked. "I was in the water... Oh—yeah. I remember now."

Fear filled his eyes, and he dropped his face into his hands.

"How did you end up in the river?"

"I didn't fall in."

"Then what happened?"

"I was thrown. I was standing near the edge, and something grabbed me from behind. It lifted me like I was nothing and tossed me into the water. I didn't hear anything, and I didn't see anything. But I know what it was."

"So do I," Smith whispered.

Lee looked up quickly, surprised.

"You figured it out?" he asked. "Do you remember what I told you before?"

"Yes, and I think I'm finally going to take your advice."

"I honestly don't know what you two are talking about," said Hastie, "but if I were you, Harrington, I'd get Lee into bed right now. We can sort out the rest later, once he's feeling better. Smith, I think we can leave him to rest. I'm heading back to college—if you're coming that way, we can talk."

But they barely spoke on the walk back. Smith's mind was spinning with everything that had happened—the mummy missing from his neighbor's room, the footsteps on the stairs, the creepy figure suddenly reappearing, and now Lee's attack, which reminded him so much of what happened to the other man Bellingham disliked. All of it started coming together in his mind, along with all the little moments that had made him suspicious of Bellingham from the start. What used to be just a strange hunch had now turned into something solid—something terrifying that he couldn't ignore.

Still, it felt unbelievable. It didn't make sense. It was too strange, too unreal—something no one would accept as true. Any judge, or even Hastie walking beside him, would probably say he imagined it all. They'd claim the mummy had never left, that Lee just slipped into the river, and that all Smith needed was rest and some medicine. And honestly, if things had been reversed, Smith might have said the same.

But now, he was sure. Bellingham was a killer, and he had some kind of weapon unlike anything anyone had ever used before in the history of crime.

Hastie split off to his own room, muttering something short about how Smith wasn't much of a talker. Smith walked across the courtyard to his own tower room, feeling sick just thinking about being there. He was sure now—he'd take Lee's advice and move out as soon as possible. How could anyone concentrate on studying when every sound from downstairs made you freeze in fear?

As he walked across the grass, he saw that Bellingham's window was still glowing with light. When he got to the stairs, the door suddenly opened, and Bellingham stepped out to look at him. His face was round and unpleasant, like an overfed spider that had just finished weaving a deadly trap.

"Good evening," Bellingham said. "Want to come in?"

"No," Smith said sharply.

"No? Still busy, I guess? I just wanted to ask about Lee. I heard something bad might've happened to him."

He sounded serious, but his eyes gave away a sneaky grin. Smith saw it—and it made him furious.

"You'll be even more upset to hear that Monkhouse Lee is doing great—he's safe now," Smith replied. "Whatever evil thing you tried didn't work. Don't act innocent. I know exactly what you did."

Bellingham stepped back, looking nervous, and half-closed the door like he was hiding behind it.

"You've lost your mind," he said. "What are you talking about? Are you blaming me for what happened to Lee?"

"Yes," Smith yelled. "You and that creepy skeleton of yours—you planned it. Listen, Bellingham. People may not burn men like you anymore, but we still hang killers. If someone else in this college dies while you're here, I'll make sure you're the one who pays. And if you don't hang for it, it won't be because I didn't try. Your weird Egyptian stuff won't work here."

"You're completely nuts," Bellingham said.

"We'll see," Smith said. "Just remember—I don't make threats I don't mean."

Bellingham slammed the door. Smith stormed off to his room, locked it, and spent most of the night pacing and smoking, thinking about all the strange and scary things that had happened.

The next day, Bellingham stayed quiet. That afternoon, Harrington dropped by and said Lee was feeling a lot better. Smith focused on his work the entire day, but by evening, he finally decided to go visit Dr. Peterson, like he'd planned the night before. A walk and a talk would help clear his head.

When he passed Bellingham's door, it was shut. But from farther down the path, Smith glanced back and saw Bellingham at the window, face pressed against the glass, staring into the night. Just getting away from him, even for a little while, was a huge relief. Smith walked faster and breathed in the fresh spring air.

The moon hung low between two tall towers, casting dark shadows on the road. A cool breeze moved the thin clouds across the sky. Soon, Smith left the buildings behind and was walking along a quiet country road that smelled like flowers.

The road to Peterson's house was quiet and not often used. Even though it wasn't late, Smith didn't pass anyone. He kept up a quick pace until he reached the gate that led to a long gravel driveway. Through the trees, he could see the warm, red light glowing from the house windows. He put his hand on the latch of the gate—but then he stopped and looked back at the road.

Something was coming.

It was creeping along the hedge, low to the ground, completely silent. Smith could barely see it in the dark, but it was moving fast. As he stared, it had already moved twenty steps closer. From the shadows, he saw a thin neck and two glowing eyes—eyes that he would never forget.

He screamed and ran up the driveway as fast as he could. The warm lights of the house were his only hope. He was a great runner, but he had never run like this before.

He heard the gate slam open behind him—the thing was coming through. There was a fast, dry tapping sound as it raced after him. When he dared to look back, he saw it bounding after him like an animal, its burning eyes locked on him and one long arm stretched forward.

Luckily, the front door was open. A sliver of light showed from the hallway. The sound behind him got louder—closer. He heard a horrible, choking sound right at his shoulder. With a cry, he threw himself inside, slammed the door, locked it, and collapsed into a chair, barely able to breathe.

"Smith! What happened?" Peterson said, stepping out of his study.

"Get me some brandy."

Peterson ran off and quickly returned with a glass and bottle.

"You really need this," he said as Smith drank. "You're pale as a ghost."

Smith set the glass down, stood up, and took a deep breath.

"I feel okay now," he said. "I've never been so terrified in my life. But if you don't mind, I'd like to stay here tonight. I can't go back out there in the dark. I know it sounds silly, but I don't care."

Peterson gave him a puzzled look.

"Of course you can stay. I'll ask Mrs. Burney to set up the spare room. But where are you going now?"

"Come with me to the upstairs window that looks at the front door. I want you to see what I saw."

They walked upstairs to a window that showed the driveway and the fields beyond. Everything looked calm and quiet under the moonlight.

"Really, Smith," Peterson said, "it's a good thing I know you don't drink. What scared you so badly?"

"I'll tell you in a second. But where did it go? Wait— look! Just beyond your gate!"

"Yes, I see," Peterson said. "Okay, no need to grab my arm that hard. I saw someone. Looked like a tall, skinny man. But what about it? And what happened to you? You're still shaking."

"I came face to face with something evil, that's what. Come back down to your study. I'll tell you everything."

He did. Under the warm glow of the lamp, with a glass of wine beside him and his cheerful, round-faced friend across the table, Smith told the full story—every strange and troubling event from the night he found Bellingham passed out in front of the mummy case up to the terrifying chase just an hour earlier.

"And that's it," Smith said when he finished. "That's the whole ugly truth. It sounds crazy, but I swear it's real."

Dr. Peterson sat quietly for a while, looking confused.

"I've never heard anything like this in my life," he said finally. "You've told me the facts. Now, tell me what you believe they mean."

"You can figure that out yourself."

"Sure, but I want to hear what you think. You've been through it—I haven't."

"Well, the details are a little fuzzy, but the main idea is clear. Bellingham, through his studies of ancient stuff, found some terrible secret that lets him bring a mummy—maybe just this one—to life for a short time. I think he was trying it the night he fainted. Even though he expected it, the sight must've shocked him. Remember? One of the first things he said was to call himself a fool. But later, he got used to it and kept doing it without fainting.

"Whatever energy he uses doesn't last long, because I've seen the mummy lying still in its case plenty of times. I believe he uses some complicated method to make it work. After figuring it out, he decided to use the thing to do his dirty work. It's strong, and it can follow orders.

"At some point, he told Lee about it. But Lee, being a decent guy, wanted nothing to do with it. They argued, and Lee threatened to tell his sister what Bellingham was really like. To stop him, Bellingham sent the mummy after him—and nearly succeeded. He'd already tested it out on another man, Norton, someone else he disliked. It's pure luck that he hasn't gotten away with two murders.

"When I confronted him, he had a big reason to get rid of me before I told anyone. He knew my habits, and he saw his chance when I left for Peterson's house. I was lucky to survive, Peterson. I don't scare easily, but I've never felt fear like I did tonight."

"My boy, I think you're taking this too seriously," Peterson replied. "You're overworked, and your nerves are on edge. Think about it—how could something like that walk around Oxford at night without being noticed?"

"It has been noticed. People in town think it's an escaped ape. Everyone's talking about it."

"It's a strange story, for sure. But even so, Smith, each part of it could have a simpler explanation."

"Even what happened to me tonight?"

"Absolutely. You left the house tired and on edge, your head full of this theory. Maybe some skinny, desperate man followed you. When he saw you run, he chased you. The rest? That's your fear and imagination filling in the blanks."

"That doesn't work, Peterson. I know what I saw."

"And about the mummy—you saw the case empty, then saw the mummy in it just moments later. But the lamp was dim, and you weren't looking closely. Maybe you just missed it the first time."

"No, that's not possible."

"And maybe Lee just fell into the river. Maybe Norton was attacked by some thief. You've got a serious case against Bellingham, but if you took it to the police, they'd just laugh."

"I know. That's why I plan to handle this myself."

"What?"

"Yes. I feel like I have a duty to act. And to be honest, it's about protecting myself too. I won't just sit back and let this thing chase me out of college. I've already decided what to do. But first, can I use your paper and pen for a while?"

"Of course. You'll find everything you need on that table."

Smith sat down with a blank sheet and started writing. For over an hour—then two—his pen flew across the pages. One after another, he filled sheets and set them aside while Peterson sat back in his chair, watching with interest. At last, Smith gave a satisfied sigh, stood up, stacked the pages, and laid the final one on Peterson's desk.

"Please sign this as a witness," he said.

"A witness? To what?"

"To my name and the date. The date is very important. My life might depend on it."

"Smith, you're talking nonsense. You should go to bed."

"Actually, I've never been more clear-headed. And I'll go to bed as soon as you've signed it."

"But what is it?"

"It's a written record of everything I've just told you tonight. I want you to sign it."

"Alright," Peterson said, signing his name below Smith's. "There. But what's the point?"

"Please keep it safe. If anything happens to me—if I get arrested—bring this out."

"Arrested? What for?"

"For murder. It's a real possibility. I need to be prepared for anything. And there's only one thing I can do now, and I've decided I'm going to do it."

"Please, don't do anything foolish!"

"Trust me, it would be far more foolish not to act. Hopefully you won't have to get involved—but it makes me feel better knowing you have this statement. And now I'll take your advice and get some sleep. I need to be ready for tomorrow."

***

Abercrombie Smith wasn't the kind of person you wanted as an enemy. He was usually calm and slow to anger, but once he decided to act, he was focused and unstoppable. The same determination that made him a great science student now fueled everything he did. He had taken a break from studying that day, but he didn't plan to waste it. He didn't tell his host what he was up to, but by nine in the morning, he was already heading back to Oxford.

In High Street, he stopped at Clifford's, the gun shop, and bought a heavy revolver and a box of bullets.

He loaded six of them into the gun, clicked it half-cocked, and tucked it into his coat pocket. Then he went to Hastie's rooms, where the big rower was eating breakfast, the Sporting Times propped up next to the coffee pot.

"Hey! What's going on?" Hastie asked. "Want some coffee?"

"No, thanks. I need you to come with me and do exactly what I say."

"Sure, no problem."

"And bring a strong stick."

"Whoa!" Hastie raised an eyebrow. "Here's a hunting crop that could knock out an ox."

"One more thing. You have a box of surgical knives, right? Give me the biggest one."

"Here you go. You look like you're going into battle. Anything else?"

"No, that's all." Smith put the knife inside his coat and led the way outside. "We're not exactly beginners anymore, Hastie," he said. "I think I can handle this alone, but I want backup just in case. I'm going to have a talk with Bellingham. If it's only him, I won't need your help. But if I yell, come running and hit hard. Got it?"

"Got it. I'll be there if I hear you shout."

"Stay right here. I might take a while, but don't move until I come back down."

"I'm not going anywhere."

Smith climbed the stairs, opened Bellingham's door, and walked in. Bellingham was sitting at his desk, writing. Beside him was the mummy case, still labeled with the sale tag 249, and the ugly mummy standing stiff inside. Smith looked calmly around the room, shut the door behind him, and walked to the fireplace. He lit a match and started a fire. Bellingham stared at him, shocked and furious.

"Well now, you're really making yourself at home," he said, stunned.

Smith sat down slowly, placed his watch on the table, pulled out the gun, cocked it, and rested it in his lap. Then he took the long knife from his coat and threw it in front of Bellingham.

"Now," Smith said, "start cutting up that mummy."

"Oh, so that's what this is about?" Bellingham sneered.

"That's right. They say the law can't stop you, but I've got my own way of fixing things. If you don't start in five minutes, I swear to God I'll shoot you in the head."

"You'd kill me?" Bellingham had stood halfway up. His face had gone pale.

"Yes."

"Why?"

"To keep you from hurting anyone else. One minute's already gone."

"But what did I do?"

"You know exactly what you did."

"This is just you pushing me around!"

"Two minutes."

"But you need a reason! You're crazy! Why should I ruin something that belongs to me? That mummy is valuable!"

"You're going to cut it up—and burn it."

"No, I won't."

"Four minutes."

Smith picked up the gun and stared at Bellingham without blinking. As the seconds ticked by, he lifted his hand, finger ready on the trigger.

"Fine! Fine! I'll do it!" Bellingham yelled.

Panicking, he grabbed the knife and started hacking at the mummy. He kept glancing nervously at Smith, who still had the gun aimed at him. Every slice made the mummy crack and fall apart. Yellow dust floated into the air, and bits of dried spices and herbs scattered across the floor. Then, with a loud snap, the mummy's spine broke, and it dropped into a pile of dry, twisted limbs.

"Now burn it," Smith said.

The fire roared as Bellingham threw in the remains. The room quickly felt like the inside of a furnace. Sweat dripped down both of their faces. Bellingham kept working while Smith sat still, watching him closely. Thick, dark smoke rose from the fire, and the room filled with the awful smell of burning hair and resin. After about fifteen minutes, the mummy was nothing but a few charred and brittle pieces.

"Happy now?" Bellingham said, glaring at Smith with fear and anger in his eyes.

"No. We're not finished yet. Everything needs to go. No more of this evil stuff. Burn those leaves too—they might be part of it."

After the leaves were tossed into the fire, Bellingham asked, "What now?"

"The scroll you had on your table the other night. I think it's in that drawer."

"No! You can't burn that!" Bellingham shouted. "You don't know what you're doing—it's one of a kind! There's knowledge in that scroll you can't find anywhere else!"

"Get it out," Smith said firmly.

"Wait, Smith—please! I'll share it with you. I'll teach you everything it says. Or just let me copy it before you destroy it!"

Smith walked over, unlocked the drawer, and pulled out the old, curled scroll. Without a word, he tossed it into the fire and pressed it down with his foot. Bellingham screamed and tried to grab it, but Smith shoved him back and stood over the fire until the scroll turned to gray ash.

"Well, Bellingham," Smith said, "looks like I've taken away your power. If you ever go back to your old ways, I'll deal with you again. Now goodbye—I have work to do."

That's Abercrombie Smith's version of what happened at Old College, Oxford, during the spring of 1884. Bellingham left the university shortly afterward and was last seen in Sudan. No one ever came forward to say Smith was lying. But people don't know everything, and nature is full of strange and hidden things. Who knows what dark secrets still wait to be found by those who go searching?

The End

Thank You for Reading

Dear Reader,

We hope this timeless classic has sparked your imagination and enriched your literary journey. Now that you've turned the final page, we want to share a vision for the future of reading—one where every classic you've ever wanted to explore is at your fingertips, in a format that best suits your life.

We'd like to invite you to gain immediate, unlimited digital & audiobook access to hundreds of the most treasured literary classics ever written—along with the option to secure deluxe paperback, hardcover & box set editions at printing cost. Together, we can spark a new global literary renaissance alongside our small, independent publishing house called "The Library of Alexandria."

Thousands of years ago, the Library of Alexandria stood as a beacon of knowledge—until it was lost to history. We aim to reignite that spirit of preservation and discovery right now, in the modern age—only this time, it's accessible to all, in every language and every format.

Picture a world where every timeless classic, novel, poem, or philosophical treatise is not only available to read but also updated for today's readers—modernized, translated into any language or dialect, and ready to enjoy in any format you choose, whether that is in an eBook, audiobook, paperback, or deluxe hardcover & box set version a printing cost.

By joining our movement to rebuild the modern Library of Alexandria, you become part of an unprecedented mission to offer:

- **Unlimited Audiobook & eBook Access to the Greatest Classics of All Time**

  Instantly explore thousands of legendary works, from Plato and Shakespeare to Jane Austen and Leo Tolstoy. All are instantly ready to read or listen to, giving you a complete literary universe at your fingertips.

- **Paperback & Deluxe Editions at Printing Costs:**

  Purchase any title in a paperback, deluxe hardbound, or deluxe boxset edition at printing costs, shipped right to your doorstep. Curate your personal library of Alexandria with editions worthy of display— crafted to last, designed to captivate, and delivered straight to your door.

- **Modern translations for Contemporary Readers in all languages and dialects**

  Discover a vast selection of classics reimagined in clear, current language—no more struggling with outdated phrases or obscure references. Next to the original versions, we aim to offer translations in as many languages and dialects as possible.

  As we continue our translation efforts and add new languages, readers everywhere can connect with these works as if they were written today. By bridging linguistic divides, you're contributing to ensuring that these timeless stories become more meaningful, accessible, and inspiring for people across the globe.

- **Your Personal Library of Alexandria:**

  Over the months and years, you'll curate a unique physical archive of classics—each volume a testament to your taste, curiosity, and love of knowledge. It's not just about owning books—it's about curating a cultural legacy you'll cherish and pass down for generations to come.

- **Join a Global Literary Renaissance:**

  Your support fuels an ongoing mission: allowing us to reinvest in offering deluxe print editions (including special boxsets) at their true cost, broaden the range of available formats and translations, and extend the reach of these works to new audiences worldwide. By joining today, you're not just preserving a legacy of masterpieces; you set in motion a powerful wave of literary accessibility.

We are more than a publisher—we're a movement, and we can't do it alone. Your support lets us scale our mission, preserving and reimagining history's greatest works for tomorrow's readers.

Become a Torchbearer of knowledge.

Thank you for picking up this book and allowing us into your literary journey. As you turn the pages, know that you're part of something larger: a global effort to keep these stories alive, share their wisdom across borders and generations, and spark a true cultural revival for the modern era.

If this resonates with you—please consider taking the next step by visiting:

www.libraryofalexandria.com

With gratitude and a shared love of knowledge,

The Modern Library of Alexandria Team

Visit:

www.libraryofalexandria.com

Or scan the code below: